Copyright © 2012 by Brun Limited

All rights reserved. No part of this book may be reproduced, transmitted, or stored in an information
retrieval system in any form or by any means, graphic, electronic, or mechanical, including
photocopying, taping, and recording, without prior written permission from the publisher.

First U.S. edition 2013

Library of Congress Cataloging-in-Publication Data is available.

Library of Congress Catalog Card Number pending

ISBN 978-0-7636-6352-0

12 13 14 15 16 17 SCP 10 9 8 7 6 5 4 3 2 1

Printed in Humen, Dongguan, China

This book was typeset in New Century Schoolbook.
The illustrations were done in mixed media.

Candlewick Press
99 Dover Street
Somerville, Massachusetts 02144

visit us at www.candlewick.com

CANDLEWICK PRESS

ANTHONY BROWNE

One Gorilla

A Counting Book

1
gorilla

2

orangutans

3

chimpanzees

mandrills

5
baboons

6
gibbons

7

spider

monkeys

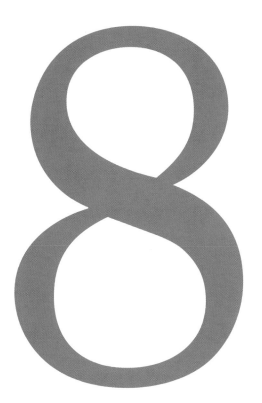

8 macaques

9

colobus
monkeys

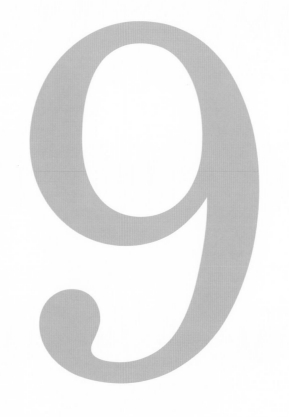

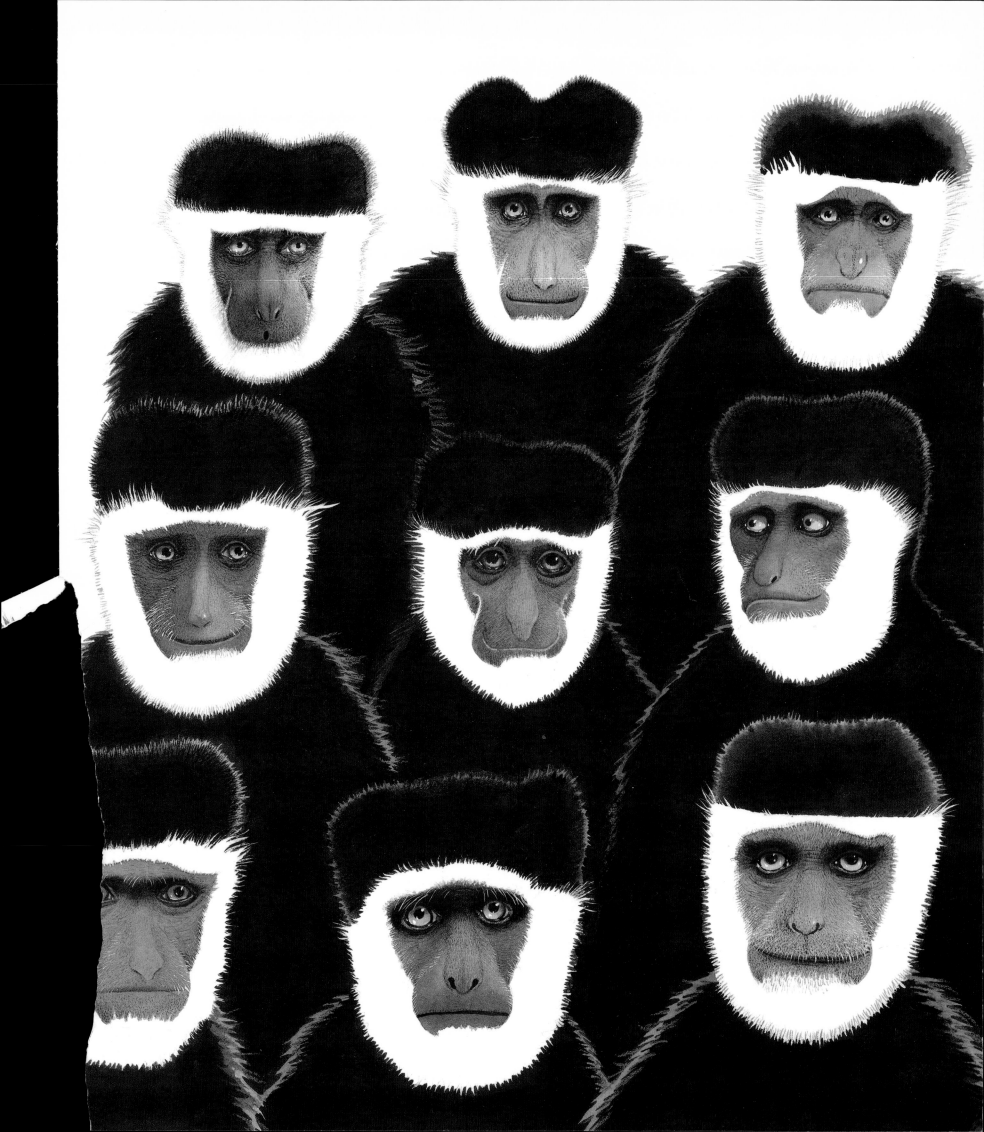

lemurs

All primates.
All one family.
All my family . . .

and yours!